Series consultant: Dr Terry Jennings

Designed by Jane Tassie

The author and publishers would like to thank Lyn Edwards, Irfan,
Sana and the staff and pupils of the Charles Dickens J & I School, London,
for their help in making this book.

A CIP record for this book is available from the British Library.

ISBN 0-7136-6196-8

First paperback edition published 2002
First published 1999 by A & C Black Publishers Limited
37 Soho Square, London W1D 3QZ
www.acblack.com

Typeset in 23/28pt Gill Sans Infant and 25/27 pt Soupbone Regular

Printed in Singapore by Tien Wah Press (Pte.) Ltd

A & C Black uses paper produced with elemental chlorine-free pulp,
harvested from managed sustainable forests.

Paper

Exploring the science of
everyday materials

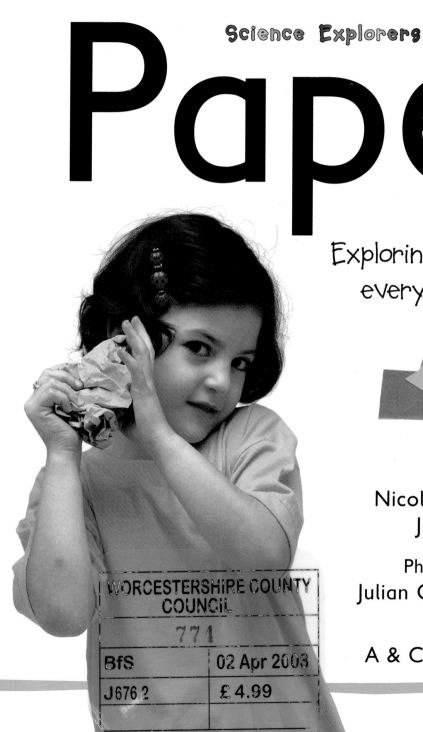

Nicola Edwards and
Jane Harris

Photographs by
Julian Cornish-Trestrail

A & C Black · London

There are lots of
different types
of paper.

3

This paper is
flat and thin.
It feels light
and smooth.

5

It's very strong.

I can't pull it apart!

7

I can scrunch it into a ball.

9

Paper's good for
drawing on.

I'm printing a pattern.

What happens when I drop the piece of paper?

It looks like it's swinging from side to side.

My scrunched-up ball of paper drops straight down.

I've made a paper plane.

Look at it fly!

What will happen
to this paper
boat if I put
it on top of
the water?

Look it floats!

I've made these boats out of different kinds of paper. I wonder if they'll float too?

Oops! I've spilled water onto this sheet of paper.
The water is sitting on top of the paper.

Look at this kitchen paper.

It soaks up the water straight away.

17

Now the paper is dry again.

It's not as
smooth as it
was before.
It looks more
crinkly.

It sounds louder when I scrunch it.

We've made a cake!

We lined the tin
with greaseproof
paper so that
the cake
wouldn't stick
to the sides.

Look how the paper has changed. It's soaked up the grease from the cake.
I can see my fingers through the paper now.

Time to tidy away.

Look at all the paper we've collected for recycling.

The paper can be used again to make new things like these.

23

Notes for parents and teachers

The aim of the *Science Explorers* series is to introduce children to ways of observing and classifying materials, so that they can discover the properties which make each material suitable for a range of uses. By talking about what they already know about materials from their everyday use of different objects, the children will gain confidence in making predictions about how a material will behave in different circumstances. Through their explorations, the children will be able to try out their ideas in a fair test.

pp2/3, 12/15

Paper is an extremely useful and versatile material. It's relatively cheap to make from the cellulose fibres found in wood pulp, and the trees from which paper is made are a renewable source.

How many different types of paper (such as tissue paper, card, blotting paper, kitchen paper, newspaper, writing paper, filter paper) can the children think of? Collect examples of all the types of paper they can name and compare them. How does each feel? How do the weights and surfaces differ? Try the activities shown in the book with different weights and strengths of paper. How do the results differ? Can the children predict which type of paper would work best, for example, for making a paper aeroplane that can fly?

Ask the children to think of everyday things which are made from paper, linking the uses to its properties, for example, what is it about paper that makes it suitable to make into cups and plates for parties and picnics?

Encourage the children to think about objects they may not have thought of as being made of paper, such as lampshades, papier mâché bowls and edible rice paper.

pp4/5

Experiment by adding a drop of vegetable oil onto the surface of an opaque piece of paper. The oil allows light to shine through to a certain extent, making the paper translucent. The children could design and make their own stained glass windows with card and tissue paper, noticing the contrasting weights and the extent to which both types of paper allow light through them.

pp6/7

Tear different types of paper and examine the fibres through a magnifying glass. The more tightly meshed the fibres are, the stronger the paper will be. To test the strength of a piece of paper, secure it over the top of a plastic bowl with a rubber band. Gently place marbles on top of the paper until it tears. How many marbles does it take before the paper tears?

Folds add strength to paper. Ask the children to try to stand a piece of paper on its edge and then fold it in half and try again. They could fold the paper into a concertina shape. What difference does it make? How many times can they fold a piece of paper in half and then in half again? Does it make any difference how large a piece of paper they begin with?

pp8/9

The children could try wrapping parcels in different types and weights of paper - which work best?

pp10/11

The children could investigate which combination of different types and weights of paper provide the best results with crayons, inks and paints.

pp16/17

The fibres in blotting paper are loosely meshed which makes the paper more absorbent. Rubbing a wax crayon over the surface of a piece of paper will make the paper water resistant.

pp18/19

Why do the children think umbrellas aren't made of paper, but some parasols are? Allowing wet paper to dry shows a reversible change, but the paper will not look sound and feel exactly the same as before. Try scrunching various types of paper. Can the children describe the different sounds?

pp20/21

Have any of the children watched paper burn? Can they describe what changes they observed? Examine paper that's been scorched or burnt and explain that the change is non reversible.

pp22/23

The cellulose fibres from which paper is made can be turned into pulp and reused. (**Paper** in the *Threads* series (A & C Black) has instructions for making paper.) Can the children think why it is important to recycle paper? If possible, take them to a paper bank, with a collection of newspapers to donate.

Find the page

Here is a list of some of the words and ideas in this book